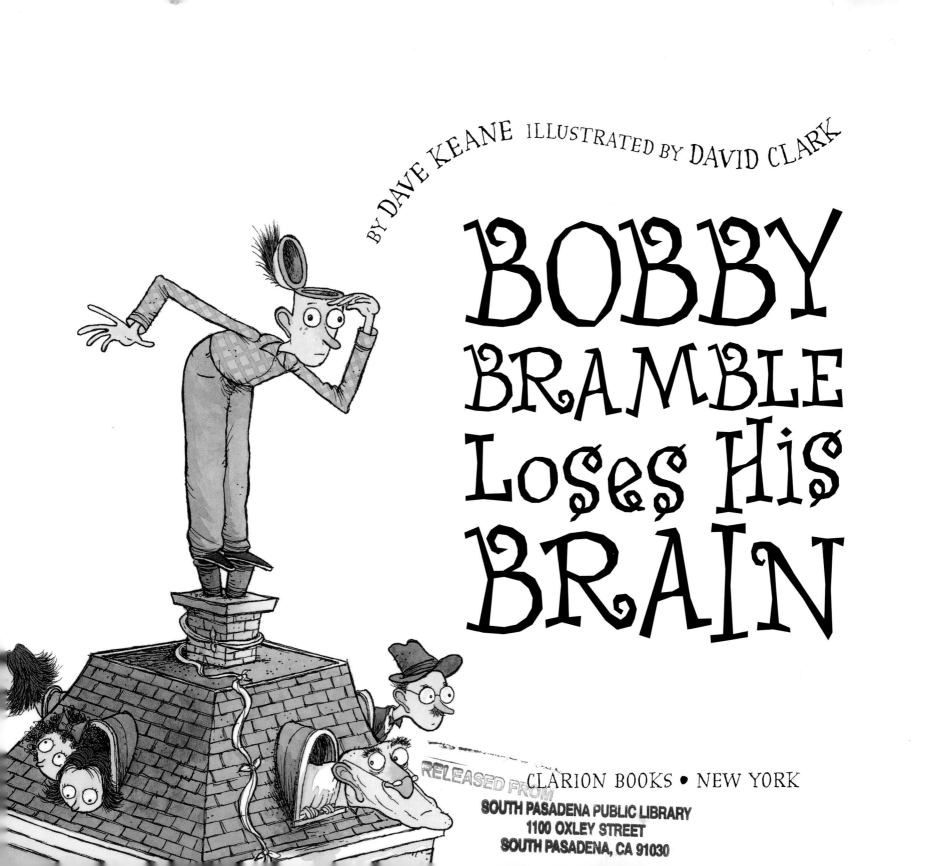

BY DAVE KEANE ILLUSTRATED BY DAVID CLARK

BOBBY BRAMBLE LOSES HIS BRAIN

CLARION BOOKS • NEW YORK

Clarion Books
an imprint of Houghton Mifflin Harcourt Publishing Company
215 Park Avenue South, New York, NY 10003
Text copyright © 2009 by David J. Keane
Illustrations copyright © 2009 by David Clark

The illustrations were executed in ink and watercolors.
The text was set in 24-point Aunt Mildred.

For information about permission to reproduce selections from this book,
write to Permissions, Houghton Mifflin Harcourt Publishing Company,
215 Park Avenue South, New York, NY 10003.

www.clarionbooks.com

Printed in Singapore

Library of Congress Cataloging-in-Publication Data
Keane, David, 1965–
Bobby Bramble loses his brain / by Dave Keane ; illustrated by David Clark.
p. cm.
Summary: Daredevil Bobby Bramble has often been warned that one day he will crack his head open,
and when he finally does, his brain escapes and runs around town as if it has a mind of its own.
ISBN: 978-0-547-05644-9
[1. Brain—Fiction. 2. Tall tales. 3. Humorous stories.]
I. Clark, David (David Lynn), 1960– ill. II. Title
PZ7.K2172Bob 2009
[E]—22
2008007245

TWP 10 9 8 7 6 5 4 3 2 1

For my son, Sutter,
whose fiercely independent mind
inspired me to write this book
—D.K.

To my family
—D.C.

Bobby Bramble was the type of boy who never used the front door.

"Bobby Anthony Bramble, get down from there!" ordered his mother. "You'll fall and crack your head open like Humpty Dumpty."

Bobby Bramble had ants in his pants, a thirst for adventure, and energy to spare.

He liked to climb, somersault, jump, bounce, slide, swing, sprint, flip, hang upside down, and generally give gravity a run for its money. He was fast and strong and brave. But no one seemed to care about that. People only worried about his head cracking open and his brains scrambling.

7

"It's bad enough having a little brother," grumbled Bobby's older sister, Becky. "But a brainless little brother would be more than I could handle."

"A mind is a terrible thing to lose," said his grandfather.

"You're really going to need your brain, Bobby," warned his little sister, Bonnie, "because you're not very pretty."

"Would everyone stop worrying about my brain?" Bobby shouted. "I'm not some kind of egghead, you know. I'm naturally hardheaded."

9

But the very next day, while Emily Filbart, the Brambles' babysitter, was busy putting on lip-gloss, Bobby's head did crack open, and his brain ran off as if it had a mind of its own.

"Hello? Mr. Bramble? This is Emily. Bobby was on the garage roof, pretending he was escaping from prison. There was a loose shingle . . . and, well, it was actually Bobby's brain that escaped."

"Officer Ryan? This is Barbara Bramble. I'd like to file a missing brain report. Yes, it's a runaway. Oh, I imagine it's gray and about seven inches tall. But apparently my son has a very quick mind, because nobody got a good look at it!"

"Barbara? Hi, it's Lorraine from down the street. Did your son finally lose his mind? I could swear I just saw it wandering around my petunias."

13

Mr. Bramble and his briefcase burst through
the front door. "Are you all right, son?" he asked
Bobby breathlessly.

"Snakes fleas ferrets! Gum apples carrots!"
Bobby blurted out thoughtlessly.

"Poor boy. He's got no brain to give his tongue directions," said Grandpa.

"He's as dumb as an onion, Dad," said Bonnie.

The neighborhood buzzed with excitement when the Channel 8 Action News van pulled up in front of the Bramble home. Before long, Bobby's father announced a twenty-dollar reward for the safe return of his son's most vital organ, no questions asked.

Mr. Dingle, the mailman, almost caught the runaway brain in his hat after it sprang out of Mrs. Frickle's mailbox.

Then Mr. Lopez, an avid fisherman, nearly netted the stray. But Bobby's brain managed to avoid capture with a slight trick of the mind.

"I've caught it!" Mrs. Baggleman cried from her vegetable garden. Upon further inspection, however, her apron yielded nothing but a rather sad-looking head of butter lettuce.

Bonnie hung up wanted posters around the neighborhood. Becky tracked sightings on a map. Grandpa set out brain traps, using flash cards as bait.

WANTED

18

But it was no use. It seemed as if they'd never get Bobby's central nervous system back into one piece, and Bobby would spend the rest of his days doing handstands and back flips without a thought in his head.

"We need someone fast and strong and brave to help us capture Bobby's brain," said Becky.

"We need someone like Bobby," said Mrs. Bramble

"Maybe we just need Bobby!" shouted Bonnie.

"C'mon, boy. Take a good whiff! Where's that brain?" hollered Mr. Bramble.

"Go get it, little fella!" prodded Grandpa. "Get that pesky brain."

Just then Bobby was startled out of
his empty-headed stare by an ear-splitting
Screeeeeech! of skidding tires. Without
looking both ways, his brain had run
into the street, just inches in front of the
hook-and-ladder truck from Firehouse 13.

Acting on gut instinct alone, Bobby shot out of the kitchen window like a cannonball—even before anyone could think to yell "Fetch!"

Bobby Bramble's body tore off after his
brain with the speed of a racehorse, the
footwork of a jackrabbit, and the dexterity
of a circus monkey.

"With moves like that, it's not too early to start thinking about playing football for the high school!" proclaimed Mayor Grubb, always mindful of appearing at newsworthy community events.

When Bobby's brain sprang over a hedge, Bobby sprang higher. When his brain zigged, Bobby zagged just steps behind. When his brain tried to outrun him, Bobby turned on the afterburners and pounced.

Like a seasoned rodeo cowboy, Bobby rode his bucking brain down the street as it jumped, jerked, and spun wildly. It was, everyone agreed, a classic battle of brain versus brawn. But finally, sensing Bobby's exceptional balance, surprising strength, and unbuckable determination, his brain came to a full and complete stop.

For three whole minutes the pair remained motionless as they came to grips with the fact that they worked better as a team.

Bobby's brain now understood that it would never get far in life without all the advantages that a body provided. And Bobby's body somehow sensed that a life without a brain would be a hollow one. Perhaps they were meant to be together.

Without thinking, Bobby popped
his brain back into his head.

A curious crowd gathered to see if the Bramble boy once again had his wits about him.

"Oh, my! He still looks goofy!" cried Bobby's mother, pushing her way through the hushed onlookers.

"Say something, Bobby," whispered his father. "Don't be afraid to speak your mind."

"MOM, CAN WE

ORDER PIZZA FOR DINNER?" Bobby suddenly bellowed, to the great relief and thunderous cheers of everyone who had witnessed the great Bramble brain scramble.

Two days later, after Bobby tried unsuccessfully to launch himself into Mrs. Baggleman's swimming pool using his backyard seesaw and a garbage can full of gravel, his brain once again tried to escape. But thanks to the football helmet that Mayor Grubb had dropped off, Bobby Bramble's brain was outsmarted.

And Bobby's been one step ahead of his brain ever since.